To Penny

Lost for a Year

Written by

Susan Hardy and Susan King

SJ Hardy Susan King

Illustrated by Sarah Wilson

Published by TwoSues Productions 2015
twosuesproductions@gmail.com
34 Church Avenue, Harrogate, HG1 4HE

A CIP catalogue record for this book is available from the British Library.

ISBN 978-0-9934433-0-5

Book layout and cover design by Clare Brayshaw

Prepared and printed by:

York Publishing Services Ltd
64 Hallfield Road
Layerthorpe
York
YO31 7ZQ

Tel: 01904 431213

Website: www.yps-publishing.co.uk

For our grandchildren:
Annabelle and Sebby – Susan K
Christopher and James – Susan H
our inspiration

With thanks to our daughters for all their help and support:
Kathryn and Sarah – Susan H
Amanda and Justine – Susan K

Months of the Year

January starts the year
February comes next
March after with a windy stir
April follows with showery zest

May at last brings warm sunshine
June arrives with flowers
July next still sunny and fine
August and lots of holiday hours

September brings cooler air
October blows the leaves
November means the trees are bare
December last but full of glees

Henry's favourite toy is Digby Pocus
A scruffy, squishy diplodocus.
He has a very long and spindly neck
His tail is blue with a little white fleck.
But Digby is lost and hidden, where only his tail shows;
Will Henry and Grandma find him … who knows?

Summer, autumn, winter, spring
Look for changes the seasons bring.

It was January and an icy day
Grandma came to Henry's house to stay.
She played with Henry and Digby too
And then they wondered what to do.

A walk in the woods is one of their favourite things
Looking at the changes that every month brings.
Henry put on gloves, scarf and a coat with a hood
He pulled on his wellies which were covered in mud.
As they both walked out of the door
Henry grabbed Digby from off the floor.

In a very cold clearing the ice was thick
The glistening wonderland played Henry a trick.
He tripped and slipped and went crashing down
Scraping his knee as he fell to the ground.
What a yelp! What a wimper! Henry's knee really hurt!
And unnoticed poor Digby fell into the dirt.

Grandma distracted Henry to soothe his pain
Spotted a squirrel track on the far terrain.
Off they trotted to follow the trail
Leaving Digby in an icy ditch, showing only his blue tail.

February brought lots of rain and sleet.
Henry put on his waterproof and wellies on his feet.
He walked towards the garden gate and heard a familiar sound
He could hear Grandma coming, her footsteps on the ground.

They wandered past the village green towards the nearby wood
They saw lots of pretty snowdrops and crocuses in bud.
A spotty red toadstool was growing beneath a tree
There was a squirrel picking pine nuts, to eat for his tea.

Grandma and Henry were having fun but had not forgotten their quest
Poor Digby was still missing and they had to do their best.
They looked high in the trees and with a wiggle and a push
Squeezed through the branches and then behind a big bush.

Where on Earth is Digby Pocus?
Can you see Henry's Diplodocus?

March came and spring was due
The sleet had gone but the north wind blew.
Grandma and Henry were dressed in snuggly clothes
They walked to the woods when they suddenly froze.

For in the distance they could see
Birds busy building nests in a large oak tree.
Daffodils nodding and crocuses covering the ground
Yellows, purple, white and greens could all be found.

There were lots of rainy puddles and muddy puddles too
Broken twigs and branches – watch out for animal poo!
But Digby was still missing; Henry hadn't forgotten his friend
He and Grandma would look for him until the very end.

Where on Earth is Digby Pocus?
Can you see Henry's Diplodocus?

April meant warmer weather was here
Grandma had a treat for Henry which made him cheer.
A treasure hunt in his favourite place!
They set off from home at a very quick pace.

When they got to the woods on their usual route
They slowed right down to search – what a hoot!
Under the bushes, left and right
Careful of baby birds but giving bugs a fright!
In among the leaves and the spring flowers
Dodging the puddles and April showers.

A red sweet, a blue toy – yummy things galore!
One, two, three, four!
Henry giggled and laughed with glee
But then thought about what he couldn't see;
His Digby was still lost – hidden away
Perhaps he'll find his friend another day.

Where on Earth is Digby Pocus?
Can you see Henry's Diplodocus?

May arrived and the sun shone bright
The pond in the wood was a wonderful sight.
Butterflies and dragonflies fluttered and flapped
Frogs croaked loudly and ducks quack quacked.

Henry caught tadpoles in his fishing net
He splished and he splashed and got awfully wet.
All of a sudden Grandma said, 'watch out Henry!'
As a great big crow swooped down in a frenzy.

Soon it was time to wander back home
Grandma and Henry's thoughts started to roam.
Digby Pocus had still not been found
They retraced their steps, eyes fixed on the ground.

Where on Earth is Digby Pocus?
Can you see Henry's Diplodocus?

Sunny June and summer arrives
Larks sing and the swallow soars and dives.
Henry and Grandma picnic in the shady glade
Egg sandwiches, jelly and lemonade.

But while flowers bloom and wildlife thrives
Grandma tries and Henry strives
To find Digby - still alone among the trees.
'At least he's warm', says Grandma and Henry agrees.

Where on Earth is Digby Pocus?
Can you see Henry's Diplodocus?

July came along, it was sunny and hot
So Grandma found a shady spot.
Under a large oak tree
Lots of mini beasts! What could they see?

There were woodlice, snails, spiders and slugs
How Henry loved to touch the bugs.
He poked and prodded at a small hole
What a surprise when up popped a mole!

Walking through the wood on their way home
Henry was with Grandma but Digby was alone.
The days, weeks and months had flown quickly by
Grandma squeezed Henry's hand and said, 'I bet he's nearby'.

Where on Earth is Digby Pocus?
Can you see Henry's Diplodocus?

August arrived hot and bright
Henry's wellies were a very clean sight!
He wore t-shirt, shorts and a white peaked hat
They marched to the wood and got tired, so they sat.
In among the cool shady trees they watched what went on
And followed trails left by animals long gone.
They imagined Digby with new woodland friends
Hidden near a path with lots of twists and bends.

Where on Earth is Digby Pocus?

Can you see Henry's Diplodocus?

September was warm with a gentle breeze
There were berries on the bushes and also in the trees.
Bees were buzzing loudly and there were flowers everywhere
Rabbits were joyfully playing and jumping in the air.

Henry found a large tree and climbed up high
'Please don't fall', said Grandma with a great big sigh.
He scrambled up the tree, it was really tough
It took him ages to get down… he'd simply had enough.

Grandma hugged Henry – they enjoyed their days together
And were happy in the wood whatever the weather.
Summer was almost over and autumn was creeping near
Henry was still hoping that Digby would reappear.

Where on Earth is Digby Pocus?
Can you see Henry's Diplodocus?

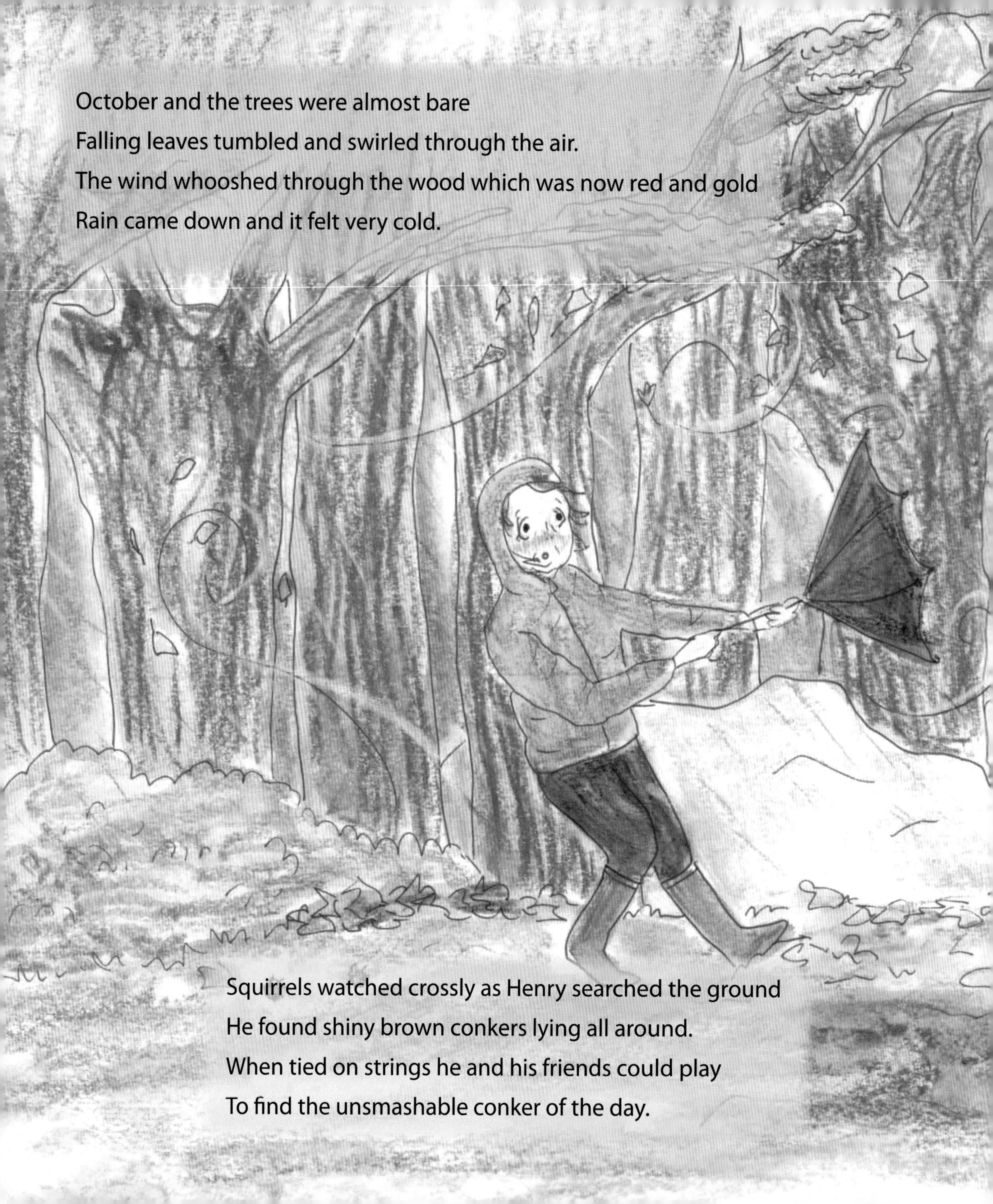

October and the trees were almost bare
Falling leaves tumbled and swirled through the air.
The wind whooshed through the wood which was now red and gold
Rain came down and it felt very cold.

Squirrels watched crossly as Henry searched the ground
He found shiny brown conkers lying all around.
When tied on strings he and his friends could play
To find the unsmashable conker of the day.

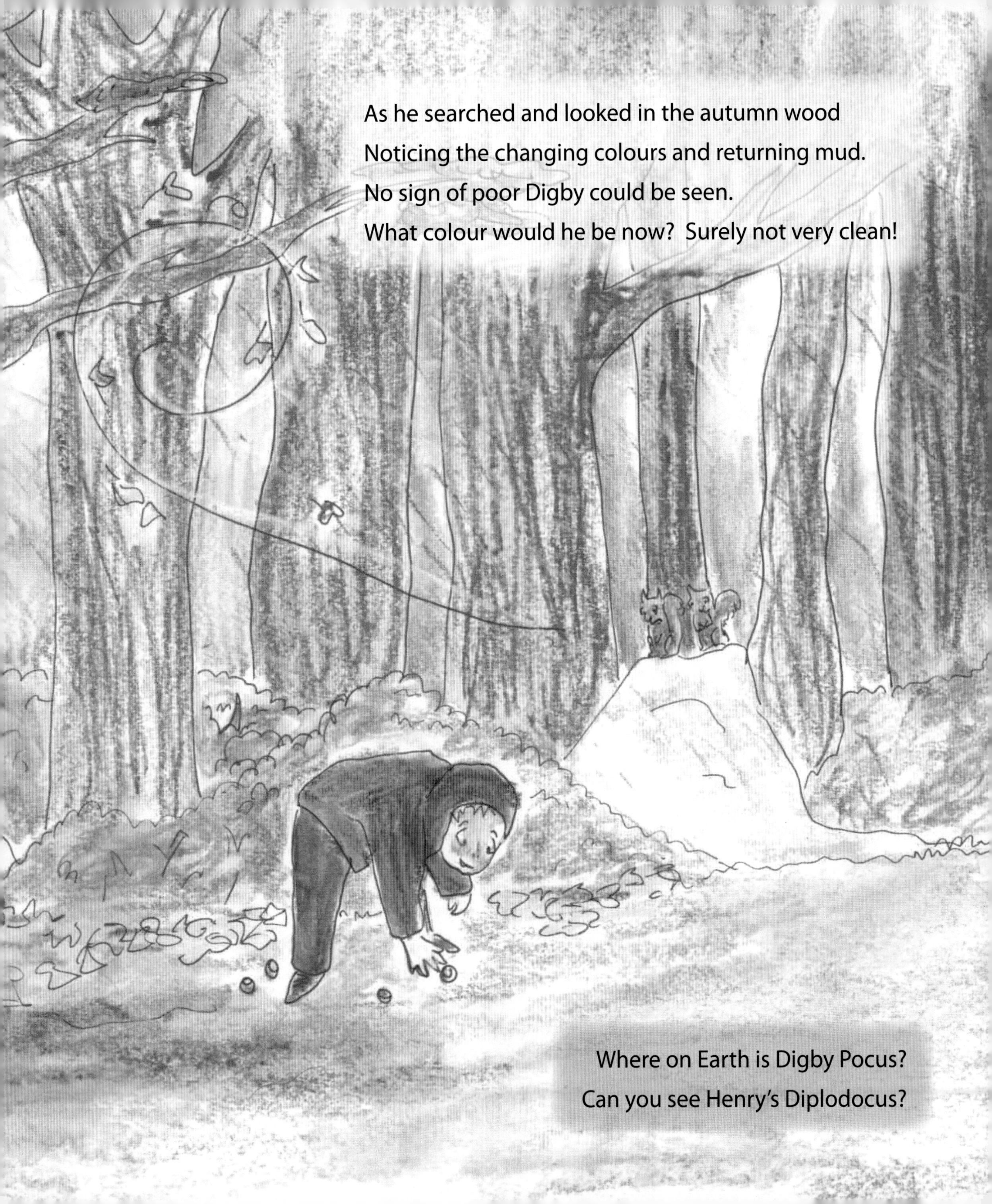

As he searched and looked in the autumn wood
Noticing the changing colours and returning mud.
No sign of poor Digby could be seen.
What colour would he be now? Surely not very clean!

Where on Earth is Digby Pocus?
Can you see Henry's Diplodocus?

November was stormy and horribly grey
The ground was boggy and the trees did sway.
Not a leaf or berry was on a tree
Nor a squirrel or rabbit could anyone see.

The birds had disappeared into their woodland nests
Shielded from the wind that was blowing from the west.
Grandma and Henry were not very pleased
They were cold and wet and had started to sneeze!

As darkness appeared it was time to go
They both walked quickly eyes on the hedgerow.
Could poor Digby survive in this weather?
Or had Henry lost him forever and ever?

Where on Earth is Digby Pocus?
Can you see Henry's Diplodocus?

December brought winter and deep, deep snow
Henry squealed with delight and was raring to go!
Into the woods they tramped crunching old leaves and twigs
Dodging low-hanging branches with frosted sprigs.

The path in the woods was soft and white
The sun shone making it twinkle bright.
Suddenly! Instantly! All at once! What did Henry see?
It couldn't be…! Could it really be?
It was scruffy and wet, tail-like and blue.
Henry ran up shouting 'Digby! It's you!'.

Here on Earth is Digby Pocus!
Henry's found his Diplodocus!